By Sam Watkins Illustrated by David O'Connell

CREATURE TEACHER

STONE ARCH BOOKS
a capstone imprint

This book is dedicated to my son Owen, a small, cheeky creature who eats mainly biscuits — S.W.

To Sarah McIntyre — D.O'C.

Creature Teacher is published by Stone Arch Books,
A Capstone Imprint
1710 Roe Crest Drive
North Mankato, Minnesota 56003
www.mycapstone.com

Published in American English in 2018 by Stone Arch Books

Creature Teacher was originally published in English in 2015. This translation is published by arrangement with Oxford University Press.

Library of Congress Cataloging-in-Publication Data is available on the Library of Congress website.

ISBN: 978-1-4965-5702-5 (Library Binding)
ISBN: 978-1-4965-5681-3 (Paperback)
ISBN: 978-1-4965-5706-3 (eBook PDF)

Summary:
Jake's class has the best teacher in the world: Mr. Hyde. There's just one teeny, tiny, HUGE problem. Mr. Hyde transforms into a naughty creature whenever he gets upset! Jake's class is desperate to keep their teacher, so they will have to use all their ingenuity to hide the creature and stop the secret from getting out!

Designer:
Mackenzie Lopez

Printed in Canada.
010407F17

TABLE OF CONTENTS

B-R-R-R-R-R-R-R-R-R-R-
RINNNNGGGGGGG-G-G-G!

The school bell screeched in Jake's ear and he leapt out of the chair with a yelp.

It's a new school, not a shark tank, he told himself, sitting once more. *But then again—what if his teacher was an old dragon? What if he didn't make any friends? What if . . .*

The office door burst open and the secretary bustled out. "I'll take you to the principal now, dear. Oops, be careful."

Jake found himself being propelled through a stream of noisy students that had erupted from nowhere. Minutes later, the hallway was empty again. The secretary stopped outside a door.

On it was a sign that read "MRS. BLUNT" in large, angry letters. Underneath, in smaller, slightly annoyed letters, it said "Principal."

"Wait here," said the secretary. "The principal will be out shortly."

A row of chairs stood along the wall and Jake perched on one. A man sat at the other end, his knees nearly grazing his ears. He wore black-rimmed glasses and was tapping a rhythm on his knee.

"MUPPETS!" he exclaimed suddenly.

Jake jumped.

The man chuckled. "Sorry. I've been trying to work out what that rhythm was and it just struck me — it's the theme from *The Muppet Show*." He looked at Jake over his glasses.

"Seeing the principal? Are you in trouble?"

"No. It's my first day," said Jake.

"Ah. I'm a new to the school too. Name's Hyde. And you are . . . ?"

"Jake Jones."

"Delighted to meet you, Jake Jones. Are you nervous?"

Jake lied. "No."

"Me neither," said Mr. Hyde. He was blushing. "How scary can the principal be, anyway? She won't bite, will she? Heh-heh."

Mr. Hyde had gone very red indeed. His face was flushed, and even his ears were scarlet. *And it even looked like . . . was he starting to . . . glow?* Jake wondered.

"If I was nervous," continued Mr. Hyde, "I would just tap a rhythm on my knee. Like this." Mr. Hyde drummed his fingers up and down gently on his leg.

Tap-tap-tappity-tap.

Jake rubbed his eyes and looked at Mr. Hyde again. He was a bit pink, but he wasn't glowing.

Suddenly the principal's door burst open and Mr. Hyde started tapping his knee furiously.

"MR. HYDE! COME IN!" a harsh voice commanded.

Mr. Hyde took a deep breath, stood up, and ducked in through the door. It clanged shut.

Jake stared at the closed door. *Had Mr. Hyde actually glowed?* He shook his head. He must have imagined it . . . *People don't glow.*

Before Jake had time to think about this, the door opened again. Mr. Hyde shuffled out, followed by a dark-haired woman in a suit. She saw Jake and frowned.

"Oh yes. The new boy. This is your teacher, Mr. Hyde. Now, let's get you both to class."

Mrs. Blunt marched them out into a courtyard with a huge pile of rocks in the middle. She stopped by the rocks, and patted one of them fondly.

"This is my Rockery. All the building work is done by students who earn three Sad Faces. A Sad Face is given for breaking one of the School Rules."

Jake's eyes met Mr. Hyde's. The rocks looked very heavy.

"Our discipline is first-rate," Mrs. Blunt continued, leading them into a hallway, her heels clicking on the hard floor. "I hope you will keep 5B in order, Mr. Hyde. They can be . . . lively."

Jake heard the sound of chatter, getting louder and louder. As they rounded a corner, he saw a gaggle of students outside a classroom door. There was pushing, shoving, and loud giggling.

"*Mrs. Blunt!*" one of the girls whispered.

The children scurried into line and the hubbub faded.

One boy dropped his lunch box and several cookies rolled across the hallway. He bent to pick them up.

"MCCRUMB!" roared Mrs. Blunt.

The boy groaned. "Maaaa'am . . .," but got back in line.

"Class 5B. Anyone wishing to work on the Rockery, continue talking. If not, go in, sit down and do not utter a sound," Mrs. Blunt ordered.

The class trooped in. Mrs. Blunt stopped the cookie-dropper.

"Barnaby McCrumb. I believe you have two Sad Faces. One more, and I will see you at the Rockery. Understand?"

"Yeeeessss, ma'am," Barnaby responded.

Mrs. Blunt glared at Barnaby, but waved him into the silent classroom and marched Jake and Mr. Hyde to the front.

"5B, meet Jake Jones," said Mrs. Blunt.

Twenty-five pairs of eyes fixed on Jake.

He would rather have been dangling upside down over a tank full of sharks.

"And this is your new teacher, Mr. Hyde. To welcome them, I want you to recite my 'Joy of School Rules' poem you've been working on for the Founders' Celebration."

There was a chorus of groans.

"QUIET! I did *not* give you permission to groan," Mrs. Blunt said.

A girl in the front row put her hand up.

"Nora?" Mrs. Blunt called on the girl.

"Ma'am, we haven't practiced for *a-a-a-ages* because Miss Read said it gave her a rash but I thought it might be a tarantula bite because tarantula hairs contain a deadly toxin —"

A boy behind Nora broke in.

"I wrote a tune for it, ma'am. Shall I sing it for you?"

"I'm not interested in songs about tarantula hair, Karl. I'm interested in Class 5B reciting my poem at the Founders' Celebration tomorrow: correct in every detail, with gusto."

She turned to Mr. Hyde.

"The Founders' Evening is an extremely important event, at which all the classes put on a performance to show their appreciation of the people who established our wonderful school and its *excellent* Rules," she explained.

She pointed to a large poster on the back wall of the classroom. At the top was written "THE SCHOOL RULES." At the bottom of the poster was a photo of the principal herself, glaring furiously out at anyone unlucky enough to be looking.

"The four remaining Founders will be attending, and parents and the local press are invited. Unfortunately, Class 5B are a *long* way behind in their rehearsals."

Her eyes bored into those of Mr. Hyde. "But under your direction, Mr. Hyde, I'm sure they will come along in leaps and bounds."

Jake saw Mr. Hyde make an uneasy smile as Mrs. Blunt turned smartly on her heels and clicked menacingly out of the classroom.

zzZZZzz
RULE 2:
NEVER
KNOW EXACTLY HOW
MANY SCHOOL RULES
THERE ARE

CLICK-CLICK-CLICK-CLICK . . . BANG!

The door slammed behind Mrs. Blunt so hard that several books leapt off the shelf in fright. Jake and Mr. Hyde jumped too.

Mr. Hyde caught Jake's eye and winked.

"First things first," he said. "Jake, you need somewhere to sit." He looked around.

"Park yourself next to the young spider scientist in the front row. Nora, isn't it?"

“Yes, sir.” She looked pleased.

Jake sat down next to Nora. She squinted at him through her glasses.

“Do you want to see my slug collection?” she asked. “I’ve got about two hundred!”

“Um,” Jake began but he was saved from answering as Mr. Hyde went on.

“Next, this poem. I’m sure you’re great! I’ll even eat my hat if you’re not amazing!” he said.

“I wouldn’t, sir,” said a boy with droopy bangs that covered half his face. “We are pretty bad. And the poem is s-o-o-ooo boring!”

Mr. Hyde clearly wasn’t prepared to believe bad of anyone or anything. He bounded around, moving desks.

“OK, everyone on the floor!” said Mr. Hyde.

Is he crazy? Jake looked around.

"Get ready, 5B! Lying down, breathe deeply!"

Slowly, the class obeyed. There wasn't much deep breathing, but Jake could hear a lot of high-pitched giggling.

After a minute of this, Mr. Hyde jumped up and stood, wobbling, on one leg, arms in the air. The class stood up and did the same.

Mr. Hyde wobbled and then fell over.

"Sir, do you want *us* to do that?" asked Nora.

He got up, straightening his glasses.

"Um, no, that's enough yoga for today," he said. "Let's hear this poem. Jake, come and be an extra pair of ears."

Jake and Mr. Hyde perched on a desk while everyone else lined up at the front. Mr. Hyde did a drum roll with his hands.

"Class 5B presents . . . 'THE JOY OF SCHOOL RULES!'" he announced.

There was nervous shuffling. Then Karl stepped forward and began:

"The School Rules make us happy,
Every girl and every boy.
We're grateful to our principal
For bringing us such joy."

Karl stepped back into line.

Jake squirmed. Karl did not look in the least bit joyful. Nor did anyone else. Mr. Hyde's smile faded slightly, but he nodded encouragingly.

After some confused whispering, a girl wearing a soccer uniform was shoved forward. She looked at Karl.

"How does my verse start?" she asked.

"The School Rules are incredible . . ."

"Oh yeah." She took a deep breath:

"The School Rules are incredible —
All one hundred and forty-two . . ."

Nora broke in. "One hundred and forty-one, Alexis! Look at the poster."

Jake looked at the School Rules poster properly for the first time. *A hundred and forty-one school rules!* He gulped. His old school had only ten! Mrs. Blunt's photo was glaring at him as if he'd broken at least half of them already.

"OK, OK . . . one hundred and forty-one . . ."

"Hang on — the poem says a hundred and forty-two," said Karl.

Nora glared at him. "What's Rule 142, then?"

"Maybe it's new," suggested Alexis.

"OK, what is this new rule, then?" Nora crossed her arms defiantly.

Karl laughed. "Rule 142 is . . . Slugs are not permitted in the classroom."

Nora frowned. “Leave my slugs out of this! They don’t do any harm — ”

“One of them slimed me yesterday,” said someone.

“One ate my salad!” called someone else. The class laughed uncontrollably.

“Calm down, everyone,” called Mr. Hyde.

No one calmed down.

“Stop hassling Nora, guys,” said the boy with the bangs.

“Woodstock, you’re only saying that because she helps you with your science homework!” someone called.

The whole class was bickering. Jake glanced around to see if Mr. Hyde was going to do something, but he had disappeared. Then —

“A-WOP-BOP-A-LOO-BOP-
A-LOP-BAM-BOOM!”

The class froze. Loud music was belting out from speakers at the front of the classroom. Mr. Hyde popped up from behind a computer.

"Zumba time!" he bellowed above the music. "Exercise will get the creative juices flowing!"

He started lurching around violently. Everyone stared, open-mouthed.

"What's he doing?" Jake heard a voice whisper nearby. Nora had slid back into her seat and was gaping at Mr. Hyde.

"Dancing, I think," he whispered back.

"5B, GET READY TO BOOGIE!" shouted Mr. Hyde. "Whatever I do, you follow. I'm warning you though, it's not easy to dance like me . . ."

A few students laughed nervously. Jake suddenly realized — Mr. Hyde was distracting the class from the argument. *Clever*!

Mr. Hyde started to clap to the music. "Join in, everyone!"

Jake nudged Nora. "Come on."

"I don't dance —"

"You do now." Jake pulled her to her feet. He started to clap. After a moment, Nora joined in. Seconds later, Alexis and Karl followed.

Mr. Hyde waggled his hands to the side. Woodstock and a few others did the same.

He shook his head. About twelve students shook their heads. Woodstock's bangs flapped madly. Nora's glasses fell off.

Mr. Hyde did the Twist — everyone twisted around! He did the Macarena, the Moonwalk, and the Monkey, the class following his every move. Woodstock did a headspin! Karl tossed Alexis in the air — which would have been more impressive if he'd caught her too.

A-WOP-BOP-A-LOO-
BOP-A-LOP-BAM-BOOM!

Abruptly, the music ended. Jake collapsed into a chair, panting. Everyone looked exhausted. Everyone except Mr. Hyde.

"Well done, everyone! You are a groovy bunch," said Mr. Hyde.

Barnaby raised his hand.

"Yes, Barnaby?" called Mr. Hyde.

Barnaby smirked. "Sir, you said that you would eat your hat if we weren't very good at reading the poem."

“And so I shall,” declared Mr. Hyde, “if we don’t get a standing ovation at the Founders’ Celebration tomorrow!”

At that moment, the bell rang. Mr. Hyde clapped his hands.

“Lunchtime! Off you go, folks. Take your time. I’ve got things I need to prepare for this afternoon.”

“What are we doing this afternoon?” asked Woodstock.

Mr. Hyde smiled mysteriously and winked. “Wait and see . . .”

RULE 3:
ALWAYS
NEVER TELL AMELIA
TROTTER-HOGG
WHAT TO DO

Jake found himself swept along in a babbling crowd of students towards the lunchroom. He heard snippets of gossip from some of his class.

". . . said he'd eat his hat!"

". . . dances like my dad."

Jake grinned. His new school was more interesting than he'd thought it would be!

There was a huge line in the lunchroom. Slowly, Jake shuffled forward till he reached the front. He grabbed a plate of spaghetti, then looked around for a seat.

Most tables looked full. Then across the hall, he spotted Nora at a table on her own. Jake walked through the chaos till he reached her. She had a plate of salad in front of her.

"Hi," he said awkwardly. "Can I sit with you?"

She looked up.

"Of course. You don't mind sharing a table with Sylvester, do you?"she asked.

She pointed at her salad. A humongous orange slug was oozing away on a piece of lettuce. Jake hesitated, then shook his head and sat down.

"No. Why should I?"

He took a mouthful of his spaghetti. "Eurrrgh!" He put his fork down. "Think I'll have the salad tomorrow," he said, looking enviously at Sylvester.

Nora nodded wisely. "Slugs know best."

Just then, the boy with the long bangs flopped in the chair next to Nora.

"Hey," he said. "Your name is Jake, right?

"Yep," said Jake. "And your name is Woodstock, right?"

Woodstock nodded. He took out a sketchbook and started to scribble.

Jake leaned over to watch.

Woodstock's scribble became a person. Glasses and a shirt turned it into Mr. Hyde. Then with some big, slick hair and sunglasses, Mr. Hyde became Elvis Presley.

Jake laughed. "That's amazing!"

Woodstock smiled. "Thanks."

Woodstock set aside his drawing.

"So, what do we think of our new teacher?" Woodstock asked.

"I like him," Nora said. "He called me a spider scientist."

"Yeah, he seems cool," said Woodstock. "Better than Mr. Sharp, anyway." He turned to Jake. "He made us clean the toilets with only our toothbrushes!"

Jake's eyes widened. "Why did he do that?"

"He's Mrs. Blunt's cousin," said Nora.

"And Mrs. Blunt," explained Woodstock, "is a horrid old dragon."

Jake laughed. "Well, I think Mr. Hyde seems really nice."

He heard a snicker, and looked around. At the next table he saw a snooty-faced girl with a ponytail staring at them. She caught Jake's eye and made a face, then started whispering to two other girls. They turned and stared at Jake.

"Mr. Hyde seems *REALLY* nice!" the girl with the ponytail mimicked in a silly voice. All the girls laughed.

Jake's face went red and he turned away.

"Who's that girl with the ponytail?" he asked Nora and Woodstock in a low voice.

"Amelia Trotter-Hogg." Nora frowned. "She's from Class 5A."

"She's also the most annoying person in the world," Woodstock added.

"Universe," Nora corrected. "She's Mrs. Blunt's pet student."

The bell rang. Jake stood up but Nora stopped him. "That's the warning bell. We still have ten minutes."

Woodstock was adding some finishing touches to his drawing.

"Finished," he said, putting his pen down.

Jake craned over to see. "Awesome. You should show it to Mr. Hyde," he said.

Woodstock grinned. "I will! You know, I think we've finally got a really amazing teacher —"

SPLOOOOOSH!

"Oops," said a sugary voice. "I accidentally spilled juice all over your *amazing* new teacher."

Jake and Nora jumped up, but poor Woodstock sat glued to his chair in shock. Juice streamed down his nose and dripped onto his drawing. Amelia Trotter-Hogg was standing behind him with an upturned cup in her hand.

"You — you —" Woodstock spluttered.

"You did that on purpose!" Nora cried.

"How would you know, goggle-girl?" Amelia said to Nora.

Jake's blood started to boil. "Hey, don't speak to Nora like that!"

"Shut up, new boy! New boys don't order me around. In fact, no one orders me arou . . ."

Amelia's voice slithered away. Jake glanced up to see Mrs. Blunt striding into the lunchroom. In an instant, Amelia changed from viper to kitten.

"Mrs. Blunt! Mrs. Blunt, hellooooo!" She skipped across the hall towards the principal.

Jake and Nora ran to get paper towels to dry the dripping Woodstock off.

"My picture's ruined," Woodstock groaned. Jake tried to cheer him up.

"It's not too bad. Actually, that splotch looks kinda cool."

"Move along, you kids. Goodness, what a mess!" A lunch lady shooed them away.

They walked back to class across the deserted playground. Well, almost deserted. Jake saw a boy crouching in a corner, candy wrappers dancing around him in the breeze.

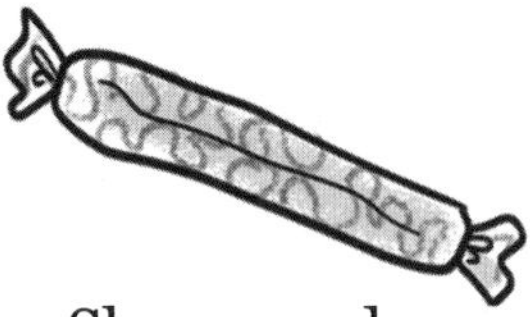

It was Barnaby. Nora saw him too. She gasped in horror.

"Oh NO! Barnaby's eating candy!" She started running towards him.

Jake looked puzzled. "So?"

"Barnaby's not allowed candy," Woodstock said. "They make him loopy."

They followed Nora.

"Barnaby, where did you get that candy?" Nora asked.

"*Nuuffink thoo dooo wiv yooo*," mumbled Barnaby through a mouthful of chocolate.

"Someone gave them to you!" exclaimed Nora. "Who was it?"

Barnaby shrugged, but his eyes slid across the playground and rested on someone for just a second too long.

Jake followed the line of Barnaby's gaze. *Amelia again!*

She was walking towards them, her two snickering friends in tow. She tossed her hair.

"Hanging out with the geeks, Barnaby?"

Barnaby scowled. "I'm not hanging out with them."

Nora rounded on Amelia.

"It was you! You gave Barnaby candy, didn't you! Why did you do that?"

"I know," said Woodstock angrily. "So he'll make trouble for Mr. Hyde!"

"Oh dear, do you think he will?" gasped Amelia in fake horror. "Poor amazing Mr. Hyde."

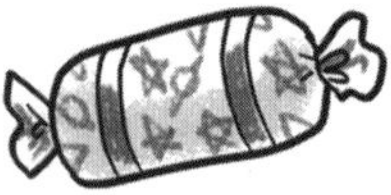

The other girls giggled. Amelia turned to Barnaby.

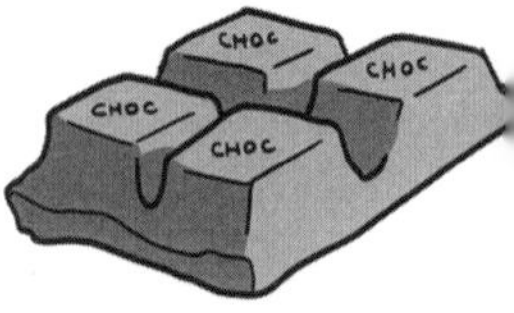

"Remember what we talked about? Bet you're too scared . . ."

She walked away, laughing.

Jake turned to Barnaby. “What did she mean? What are you too scared to do?”

Barnaby jumped up, wiping chocolate from his mouth.

“I’m not scared of anything. I’m Barnaby McCrumb! Teachers beware, the McCrumb Menace is ready for battle!”

He raced off, a crazed look in his eyes.

MINT
CHOC
CHOC
CHOC
CHOC

RULE 4:
DESTRUCTION OF THE SOLAR SYSTEM IS
REQUIRED
STRICTLY FORBIDDEN

Nora groaned. “He’s going to be a nightmare.”

“Will he really be *that* bad?” asked Jake. “It’s just a little bit of candy.”

“Last time he ate candy he rode a cleaning cart around the school and crashed it in the pond,” said Nora grimly.

“The time before he climbed on the roof and made monkey noises,” said Woodstock.

"Then he got stuck. Miss Read had to call the fire station."

"OK, maybe you're right," said Jake. "We'd better get back to class quick, then!"

They ran across the playground and back to the classroom. A crowd of students was jostling at the door. Barnaby was nowhere in sight.

"What's happening?" Jake asked a girl. She pointed at a sign on the door.

Journey? The talking petered out. Mr. Hyde had appeared in the doorway.

"Class 5B, your spaceship awaits . . ."

Alexis went first. "Ooooooh," she gasped.

The next student went in. "Aaaaaaah."

Jake stepped through the door. It was dark, so it took a moment for his eyes to adjust. He looked up. “Wow!”

Around the ceiling hung glowing globes. Some of them were greenish-blue, others fiery orange and red. One even had rings around it. *The planets!* In the middle hung the largest and brightest of all — the sun.

Everyone gaped in stunned silence. Mr. Hyde gave them a minute to take it in. Then he stood up, holding a plate of cakes.

“Greetings, Earthlings,” he cried. “Observe our wondrous solar system! I’ve even made my special moon rock cakes!”

Just then the classroom door burst open.

Barnaby! Jake froze. *Would he make a scene? Would he make trouble for Mr. Hyde?* But Barnaby just sauntered to his desk and flung himself onto his chair.

"You nearly missed lift-off!" said Mr. Hyde. "Now, where were we? Oh yes. Of course the moon is not *actually* made of cake."

RUSTLE, RUSTLE.

Jake looked around. Barnaby was rummaging in his bag.

"Stop it," Nora hissed.

Barnaby stopped. Jake glanced at him. He seemed to be listening intently to Mr. Hyde. Maybe he was going to be OK, after all. No, Jake saw a glint in Barnaby's eyes. What was he up to?

". . . some believe it was created when a large asteroid hit Earth," continued Mr. Hyde.

Faster than a speeding asteroid, Barnaby whisked a paper plane out of his bag and launched it straight at Nora! Jake watched in horror as it flew through the air. The paper plane missed Nora, did a ninety-degree turn, and landed right in the middle of Mr. Hyde's platter of moon rock cakes.

Jake held his breath. Mr. Hyde would get mad!

But Mr. Hyde picked up the plane, dusted the crumbs off and examined it.

"Nice plane, Barnaby," he said, "But not designed for a moon landing."

Barnaby gaped at Mr. Hyde in disbelief. *Barnaby thought that would make Mr. Hyde angry*, Jake realized. But Mr. Hyde just continued on.

"Which reminds me. On July 21st, 1969, the world held its breath as Neil Armstrong prepared to become the first human on the moon!"

With dramatic breath-holding and even a bit of moon walking, Mr. Hyde acted out the lunar landing. He made it seem almost real! Jake could imagine everything, and felt as if he actually *was* Neil Armstrong, taking one small step.

All eyes were focused on Mr. Hyde as he picked up a remote control. He pointed it at the ceiling. With a shudder, the planets started to revolve, moving faster and faster.

"Oooooooooh!" said the class, as one.

Mr. Hyde walked among them, explaining, "The planets move around the sun in a spectacular planetary dance . . ."

"YIPPEEEE-KI-AYEEEEE!"

Jake whirled around just in time to see a wild-eyed Barnaby jump on his desk and make one giant leap straight for Mars! Barnaby caught hold of it, and was whisked through the air straight for Jake. Jake ducked, and Barnaby's feet just missed his head.

"Yabba-dabba-doooo! Planet Barnaby coming throoooough!" he shouted gleefully, spinning around the classroom.

The solar system creaked horribly. Mr. Hyde frantically stabbed at the remote control to stop it, but it sped up! Barnaby didn't look so happy to be joining in the planetary dance now.

"MAKE IT STOP!" he screamed, clinging on to Mars for dear life. Students scrambled to get out of the way of Barnaby's flying feet, but Alexis was too slow and he thwacked her on the head.

"OW!" she cried. "Barnaby!"

She grabbed one of his dangling legs. Then she pulled on it as hard as she could.

The solar system pulled the other way, as hard as it could.

Something had to give.

Creeeeeeeeeeaaaaaaaaaak . . .

CRACK! Jake scrambled under his desk.

CRASH!

"Planet Barnaby" and the entire solar system crashed down onto the classroom floor.

There was a horrified silence. Jake lifted his head up.

Bits of planet lay around the room. Mr. Hyde stood shell-shocked in the middle of the chaos, Saturn's rings around his neck.

As he slowly removed them, Jake saw his face turn almost as red as Mars. Soon, even his ears were deep red.

Jake stared. Mr Hyde was glowing. Just like Mr. Hyde had glowed outside the principal's office that morning. *So I didn't imagine it!* And what was that weird smell . . . sort of like burning rubber?

"Are . . . are you OK, sir?" whispered Nora.

Mr. Hyde didn't answer. He glowed even brighter, from the tips of his hair to his feet. Barnaby snickered. The rest of the class sat in petrified silence. They had seen many teachers go red, some who had run screaming from the classroom, and one had been taken away in an ambulance. But none had ever lit up like a firework before!

By now, Mr. Hyde was glowing so brightly that Jake couldn't bear to look at him. Jake closed his eyes . . .

BANG!

Then a popping sound. Like fireworks.

Wheeeeeeee . . . . like air escaping from a balloon.

And finally, what sounded suspiciously like a VERY loud fart.

RULE 5:
YOU MAY
NEVER EAT PURPLE
POWDER PAINT
AND BOGIES

Jake slowly opened one eye, then the other, and felt his jaw drop.

Where Mr. Hyde had been standing, there was a cloud of purple smoke. Mr. Hyde was nowhere to be seen.

There was a sudden whoop. Jake whirled around. It was Barnaby.

"Round One to me! I knew I could break him!"

"Be quiet, Barnaby," said Jake shakily.

Barnaby grinned. "That was epic!"

Jake glared at him. "No, it was mean." He stood up, took a deep breath and stepped cautiously toward the slowly dispersing cloud of smoke. "He's gone!"

All eyes were on Jake. He realized they expected *him* to do something. *Great.*

He looked around. *Where could Mr. Hyde be? He couldn't have vanished into thin air!* Then he heard a scuffling noise behind the teacher's desk.

"Mr. Hyde?" Jake peered around the desk.

Nothing. Just a moldy old banana skin.

Scuffle scuffle.

Jake leaned over and looked under the desk.

Nothing. No, wait. *What was that?*

In the corner, Jake saw a fleck of light. He looked again. Eyes! Little glittering eyes!

Squatting under the desk was a small, hairy creature. And it was wearing Mr. Hyde's glasses!

The creature stared curiously at Jake.

"Eeeee?" it squeaked.

Jake realized his mouth was hanging open. He shut it.

"Jeeper-jeeper-jeeper-jeeper-jeeper!" chattered the creature.

Then it swung onto the desk and blew the longest, loudest raspberry Jake had ever heard. He thought it could even have made it into *The Guinness Book of World Records*.

It went on . . . and on . . .

Finally, it stopped.

Someone snorted. Someone else giggled. Within moments, the whole class was roaring with laughter.

The creature giggled and blew several smaller raspberries as an encore. Then it flew into the air like a poorly behaved missile.

SPLAAAAAAT!

It landed on Woodstock's desk.

"Arghhhh!" Woodstock yelped, and hid behind his bangs.

"Arrghhh?" The creature hid behind its bangs.

Woodstock couldn't help but laugh. Then the creature saw a piece of paper sticking out of Woodstock's bag.

"Eeeee?" It pulled the paper out. It was the drawing of Mr. Hyde, still soggy with fruit juice. It nibbled a corner.

"Mmmmmm . . ."

"Hey!" Woodstock made a lunge for the creature but it was too quick for him. It grabbed

Woodstock's ruler and used it to pole-vault off the desk.

Alexis and Karl dove under the desk as it flew towards them. It crash-landed on Karl's desk, sending pens and pencils flying. Then the

creature scampered madly across the desks to the back of the classroom

Students scattered, giggling, as it bounded towards them. This was definitely the funniest, most exciting lesson they'd ever had!

The creature screeched to a halt in front of the School Rules poster. It stared at the poster with great interest. Jake had not read all the rules, but they included the following:

NOTICE
DO NOT CLIMB ON THE DESKS.
DO NOT LAUGH.
DO NOT PICK YOUR NOSE.
IF YOU HAVE ALREADY PICKED YOUR NOSE,
DO NOT EVEN THINK ABOUT EATING IT.

The photo of Mrs. Blunt below the rules looked even more mad than usual.

With a wild look in its eye, the creature laughed. It picked its nose and ate the bogey. (The creature really didn't look as if it thought much about it, admittedly.)

Then it spotted a can of purple paint sitting on the table below the poster. It stuck its head in the can. Half a second later, its head came back out, looking purple and surprised.

"A- a- a- a- aaaaaaaaaaaaaaaa CHOOOOOOOOO!"

Purple powder paint mixed with snot sprayed all over the School Rules poster.

Everyone gasped. Mrs. Blunt was now wearing a large purple moustache, thick purple eyebrows, and purple hair. A huge bogey was stuck to her nose. Barnaby laughed so hard he fell off his chair.

Jake had to grin. Mrs. Blunt somehow looked nicer with a purple moustache and eyebrows. He looked around for the creature, but it had vanished.

Karl, Alexis, Woodstock, and Nora ran over. They all started talking at once.

“Where’s it gone?”

“What *is* it?”

“Where’s Mr. Hyde?”

“I think I know,” said Jake. They looked at him.

“It’s wearing Mr. Hyde’s glasses. I . . . I think that creature IS Mr. Hyde!”

Nora’s eyes almost popped out. “What – ?”

From the ceiling came a squeak. The creature was hanging upside down on a light fixture and stuffing purple paint into its mouth. It flung the empty can away.

BUUUUURRRRRPPP!

They stared up at the dripping purple fur ball.

“It’s eaten a whole can of paint,” said Nora, concerned. “That can’t be good for it.”

“If it is Mr. Hyde, we need to catch it before Mrs. Blunt comes back,” Jake said quickly. “She’ll definitely fire Mr. Hyde if she finds out he's turned into a creature!"

"But how?" Karl asked.

"I'll climb up and tackle it," Alexis said.

"No way," said Nora. "We should research what sort of creature it is. I'll get the Animal Kingdom book —"

"We've got to catch it first," said Jake quickly. "I'll do that. Alexis, stand guard outside the door. Make sure to watch out for Mrs. Blunt. Everyone else, tidy up the room!"

Barnaby walked over.

"I'll help you catch it," he said, grinning.

Jake frowned. He didn't trust Barnaby. But he didn't have time to think about it because Alexis burst back into the classroom.

"MRS. BLUNT'S COMING!"she yelled.

The class sprang into a cleaning frenzy. Jake began to climb on to the desk below the creature.

"No need for that," said Barnaby.

Jake stared at him. "Why not?"

Barnaby pushed Jake to one side and held an open sports bag underneath the creature.

It swayed and moaned.

Then it barfed purple paint.

Mostly over Jake.

It let go of the light, and fell.

Right into Barnaby's bag. In a flash, Barnaby zipped it up.

Jake quickly wiped himself down.

"CLASS 5B. WHAT ON EARTH IS GOING ON?"

Mrs. Blunt really was in a very bad mood indeed.

RULE 6:
BURP
ALWAYS ~~BE QUIET~~ IN
THE PRESENCE OF THE
PRINCIPAL

"You have three seconds to return to your seats. One . . . two . . ."

Jake slid into his seat just in time. Mrs. Blunt's piercing eyes swept the class. They fell on Nora.

"Nora Newton. Where is your teacher?"

"Um, he went to the storeroom, ma'am."

"I shall wait for him, then," said the principal, crossing her arms.

She suspects something, Jake thought.

Mrs. Blunt started to stalk around the classroom, scrutinizing the work on the walls.

Jake shot upright. *The School Rules poster!* Mrs. Blunt would see the purple moustache and eyebrows. He raced to the back of the room, reaching the poster seconds before Mrs. Blunt.

"What are you doing, boy?" she snapped.

"Errr . . . it's a lovely day isn't it?" blurted Jake.

Mrs. Blunt glared at him. "No, it is not. Now sit down before I give you a Sad Face."

Nora ran over and stood next to him. "Ma'am, do you want to see my slug collection?"

Mrs. Blunt looked ready to implode. "Back to your seats THIS INSTANT, unless you both want to work on the Rockery after school!"

Nora threw Jake a scared look. If they moved, she would see the poster. If they didn't . . .

"BUUUUURRRRRRP!"

Jake gasped! The burp had come from Barnaby's bag. Mrs. Blunt's eyebrows shot up.

"BARNABY MCCRUMB!" she roared.

Barnaby looked huffy. "It wasn't m—" He stopped. Everyone glared at him. He shoved his bag under the table with his foot. "It wasn't . . . my loudest burp, ma'am!"

He opened his mouth and burped. A truly magnificent burp.

In three strides, Mrs. Blunt was at the front of the classroom.

"Barnaby McCrumb. You've earned yourself an hour's work after school on the Rockery. Class 5B, when Mr. Hyde returns, please inform him that I expect your performance tomorrow night to be the best in school. Otherwise . . ."

She jostled Barnaby out of the classroom. Everyone started talking. Karl thumped Jake on the back. "I'd forgotten about the poster!"

"Never mind the poster. Where's Barnaby's bag?" Jake asked anxiously.

Alexis ran to Barnaby's desk. "Here!" She pulled it out. "Do you really think that thing is Mr. Hyde?"

An excited crowd gathered around Alexis. She unzipped the bag a tiny bit and peered inside. A furry arm shot out and grabbed her nose.

She zipped it up again hurriedly.

"You'll scare him! Give him to me." Nora pushed her way through the crowd of classmates and grabbed the bag. "There, there," she soothed it. "Now we need to find out what he eats."

"Maybe slugs?" said Karl, slyly. Everyone laughed.

"KARL!" Nora screeched.

If they start yelling, Mrs. Blunt'll be back, thought Jake. He ran to Mr. Hyde's desk and rapped loudly. Everyone looked at him.

"YOWWWW!"

"Be quiet and listen, everyone! This is important. No grown-ups can know about Mr. Hyde turning into a creature. And no one from any other class. This has to be our secret. Otherwise Mr. Hyde will be fired."

"And we'll get another Mr. Sharp," added Woodstock.

There was a chorus of groans.

Nora stood up. "Everyone has to swear an oath –"

At that moment, the bell rang for the end of school. There was a stampede for the door.

"Wait, you haven't sworn," Nora pleaded, but it was no good. Soon the only ones left were Jake, Nora, Woodstock, Karl, and Alexis.

"Now what?" asked Alexis.

Woodstock clapped his hands. "Let's take him to your tree house, Nora!"

Jake's eyes widened. "You've got a tree house?"

Nora nodded. "Yes, but it's Top Secret, so you can't tell anyone. Only Woodstock, Karl, and Alexis know about it. And now you. OK, we'll take him there."

"I can't — I've got soccer practice," said Alexis.

Karl jumped up. "And I've got a guitar lesson. Sorry, got to go!"

They both ran off.

Jake picked up the bag with Creature inside and headed out of the classroom with Nora and Woodstock. As they walked past the Rockery, they saw Barnaby struggling under the weight of a huge rock.

Jake stopped, feeling bad. "Barnaby!" he called.

Barnaby threw his rock down, wiping sweat from his forehead.

"That was a great burp," said Jake. "Sorry you got in trouble for it."

Barnaby shrugged. "Whatever. Can I have my bag?"

Jake shook his head. "The creature's still in there."

"I'll take him home . . ." Barnaby stretched out a hand.

Jake pulled it away. "No, we're taking him to —" He remembered he wasn't supposed to mention the tree house.

"Aw, come on. It's my bag!"

"Sorry, Barnaby."

"Hey, Jake!" Woodstock yelled.

Jake turned around. Nora and Woodstock were standing outside one of the windows to the main hall, waving at him. He ran over.

"What? What is it?"

Woodstock pointed to the window. "In there . . ."

Jake peered in. His eyes nearly popped out.

Amelia was prancing around the stage wearing a black leotard, pink fluffy head boppers, and pink sheets attached to her arms. A ragged line of students trailed behind her, also in costume. A tinny song piped over the speakers.

"Tra-la-la, tra-la-la!
Come one and all to the Butterfly Ball!"

Jake realized that they were supposed to be insects. Amelia was presumably a butterfly. Her two friends were smug-looking bees. He also identified a sulky spider, a caterpillar made of four students under a sheet, and several confused ants who kept tripping over each other.

"They're terrible!" whispered Nora gleefully.

Jake nodded. But, wait a second . . .

"Uh-oh." He pointed.

Just in front of the stage sat Mrs. Blunt.

"Fabulous fluttering, Amelia!" she called. "Ants, stay in line, please!"

The friends turned and started walking slowly away from the school.

"That does it," said Woodstock gloomily. "Mrs. Blunt will think they're great, since she's helping them practice."

"We've *got* to be the best at the Founders' Celebration," said Nora. "Or she'll get rid of Mr. Hyde."

They looked at the bag in silence.

"She'll definitely get rid of him if he's a creature," said Jake. "Come on, let's get him to the tree house. Then we'll have to try and get him to change back."

RULE 7:
REMEMBER TO
ALWAYS GO ~~UNDER~~ OVER
THE FALLEN TREE

"Here we are," said Nora.

Jake nearly collapsed on the sidewalk in relief. The bag was very heavy. He looked up at the huge, rambling old house that Nora had stopped outside.

"You live here?" he said, surprised. "My house is just up the road."

"Cool! And I live just around the corner," said Woodstock. "We can walk to school together, if you like." He started opening the gate. Nora stopped him.

"We'll go around the back. Dad's doing important work today," she said, cryptically.

"Saving the planet?" asked Woodstock, grinning.

Nora gave him a look. "Maybe."

She led them up an overgrown alley, stopping at a green gate.

"Keep close to me," she warned. "Step where I step. Don't touch anything. Don't make sudden movements —"

Jake giggled. "Can we breathe?"

"Yes, but quietly. I've got . . . security devices."

"Booby traps," Woodstock whispered.

Jake's eyes widened.

"Stick close to me and you'll be OK."

Nora smiled reassuringly at Jake as she pushed the gate open. Jake didn't feel reassured.

They stepped through the gateway.

Jake whistled. Monstrous plants towered over him, with flowers that looked like they could eat you alive! Nora set off through the dense undergrowth, shouting instructions. Jake tried to keep up, but he was slowed down by the bag. Soon she was completely out of sight.

Her voice floated back faintly.

". . . around the puddle . . . under the fallen tree . . ."

"Wait!" Jake shouted. "Under or over?"

No reply.

Woodstock crawled up behind him.

"Over," he said.

Jake heaved the bag up and started to climb over the fallen tree.

"UNDER!" came a shout from over his head.

Jake threw himself backward, landing on Woodstock. Woodstock yelped. The bag slid down and landed on Jake's head. Jake and the bag squawked. The boys picked themselves out of a pile of dead leaves, groaning.

Jake shook a roly-poly bug out of his ear and glared at Woodstock.

"Over?" Jake said.

"Sorry," said Woodstock, rubbing his head.

They crawled under the log.

"Up here!" Nora's voice floated down from the treetops. Jake looked up. Perched at the top of an enormous tree was a tree house. A rope ladder and assorted cables snaked up the trunk. He slung the bag over his shoulder and started to climb.

Every muscle in Jake's body screamed as he climbed, and he could hear frightened squeaks coming from the wildly lurching bag. Gasping for breath, he reached the hatch. It flew open and Nora reached down, grabbing the bag from him.

"Thanks," Jake panted, hauling himself through.

He stood up and gasped.

Test tubes full of gross liquids lurked in one corner and something gruesomely green gurgled away in a glass beaker. A rickety bookcase leaned against the wall, stacked with hefty books with titles like *Learning to Love Gravity* and *Rocket Science for Beginners*.

Nora smiled proudly. "Welcome to my laboratory!"

Woodstock's bangs flopped up through the hatch, followed by the rest of him. They stood looking at the whimpering bag.

"We should let him out," Nora said. "He's not happy."

"OK," said Jake. He spoke to the bag.

"Mr. Hyde . . . um . . . Creature? I'm going to let you out. Try to be good, OK?"

The bag twitched.

Nora leaned over. “And don’t eat my experiments. They aren’t good for the tummy.”

The bag grunted.

Jake held his breath and unzipped the bag.

For a moment, nothing happened. Then . . .

“YIPPPEEEEEEEEEEEEEEE!”

Creature rocketed into the air. Jake fell over backward. There was a rattling, and a shower of dust. Then silence. Jake peered around. Where’d he gone? Aha — there he was, crouching on a beam in the roof.

“OK,” Jake said, eyeing him nervously. “We’ve got to turn Creature back into Mr. Hyde before tomorrow night.”

“By the morning, really,” said Nora. “So we can practice the poem.”

“Yeah, but how?” asked Woodstock, twiddling his bangs thoughtfully.

Nora took a medical encyclopedia from the bookshelf and started flicking through it.

"What made him change in the first place?" Jake said.

"Maybe it's an allergic reaction," said Nora, pointing to a picture in the book.

Woodstock shook his head. "An allergic reaction gives you a rash; it doesn't turn you into a crazy creature!"

There was a cackle from the ceiling. They looked up. Creature was gleefully swinging from the lightbulb like a trapeze artist. He let go, flew through the air, and landed on the bookcase, causing it to wobble dangerously. *Learning to Love Gravity* slid off, fell through the air, and landed — *WHUMP!* — on Woodstock's head.

Woodstock yelped, "OW!"

"You'll wreck my tree house!" Nora's cheeks were turning red with anger.

A lightbulb went on in Jake's brain. "Hey," he said. "Your face is turning red."

"Is it?" Nora put her hands to her cheeks.

"It's great," Jake said. "It's sort of what happened before Mr. Hyde changed. Barnaby wrecked his solar system. He got really angry —"

Nora clapped her hands. "Of course! When he gets angry he changes into Creature!"

"Would making him happy change him back, then?" Woodstock wondered. He pulled out his sketchbook and started scribbling.

"What are you drawing?" Jake peered over.

Woodstock held up his picture: a grinning Creature lounging by a swimming pool, wearing sunglasses and slurping a huge ice cream.

"That's a good idea. Show it to him," said Nora. "It might make him change back."

Woodstock nodded his head, then waved his sketch around.

"Creature! I've drawn your portrait!" Woodstock called. No answer. Creature had disappeared again. "Where's he gone?"

Nora gave a shriek.

Creature was squatting among the items on Nora's desk. He was clutching two test tubes. One tube was full of green goo, and the other one fizzing with some orange stuff.

"My stink bomb!" Nora cried in horror.

Jake and his friends prepared to dive on the giggling Creature.

"HEE-EE-LLLLPPPPPPPP!"

Jake and Woodstock froze. A scream had come from below the tree house. Milliseconds later, a red light by the door started flashing and a siren wailed. Creature dropped the test tubes and shot behind the bookcase, mumbling in fright.

"What's happening?" shouted Jake, hands over his ears.

Nora walked calmly to the door and switched off the siren. She smiled grimly.

"*Someone* got caught in my trap!"

RULE 8:
TELL ~~NO~~ EVERY ONE ABOUT
THE TOP SECRET
TREE HOUSE

The two boys raced to the window, but it was hard to see anything through the leaves. Jake turned to see Nora fiddling with an ancient TV.

"It's hooked up to a camera," Nora explained. "It'll show us who's in the trap."

A fuzzy image appeared on the screen. Jake held his breath. As the picture flickered into focus, Jake saw a figure yelling and thrashing about in a net hanging three feet off the ground.

"Barnaby!" they all exclaimed together.

"What's he doing sneaking around in my yard?" Nora asked, angrily.

They looked at the screen. Barnaby's arms and legs were poking out of the net, like a fly caught in a huge web. Woodstock giggled. Jake and Nora started laughing too.

"Not yabba-dabba-doo-ing now, is he?" Woodstock grinned. "Shall we leave him there?"

"Tempting, but I'll have to let him out," said Nora. "You two go down while I lower the net and keep an eye on Creature."

Jake and Woodstock clambered down the ladder to the struggling Barnaby. As they reached the bottom, Jake heard a loud *CLUNK* from the tree house. The net and Barnaby crashed heavily to the ground in an explosion of dirt and leaves.

Barnaby crawled out of the net and stood up, dripping with mud and covered in leaves from head to foot. He shook his head, dislodging a family of roly-poly bugs from his hair. Jake and Woodstock had to laugh.

"Yeah, yeah, very funny!" Barnaby fumed. "I've just had to lug about two million stupid rocks from one side of the school to the other and now you guys are trying to kill me!"

"Sorry," said Jake, trying to keep a straight face. "But you did look funny."

"What are you doing in Nora's yard, anyway?" asked Woodstock.

"I wanted to help you with the creature," said Barnaby. He adjusted his messy glasses.

"But how did you know to come here?" asked Jake.

Barnaby laughed. "Easy. Nora's always going on about her not-so-secret *Top Secret* tree house! I knew you'd bring him here."

Jake sighed. "Well, now you're here I suppose you might as well come up."

They helped Barnaby out of the net and climbed back up the ladder. Barnaby went first. When he got to the hatch, Nora was there to greet him with an icy glare.

"Say the password," she snapped.

"I don't know the password."

"Well then, you can't come in." She crossed her arms.

"Nora, let him in," Jake called up. "He's soaking wet. And I know he will say sorry for sneaking around. *Won't you*, Barnaby?" Jake looked at Barnaby with a serious stare.

"Oh . . . yeah. Sorry."

"Well," Nora relented, "OK. For five minutes. But don't touch anything. And you'll have to swear an oath —"

But Barnaby had already scrambled up into the tree house. His eyes lit up.

"Whoooaa, awesome clubhouse!"

"It's not a clubhouse, it's a laboratory," said Nora, persnickety as ever.

He walked over to the desk with all the test tubes on it.

"These are so cool! What's in here?" He picked up a flask and shook it.

"That's my homework!" Nora grabbed it from him.

Barnaby put his hands up. "OK, calm down! So where's the creature, then?"

Jake had almost forgotten about Creature in all the excitement. He ran to look behind the bookcase. Creature's eyes glittered in the shadows, but when he saw Jake he hissed and his hair stood on end. He scrambled up the shelves and squatted on the top, twittering.

"Come down, Creature," said Jake. Creature didn't move.

"He was scared by the siren," said Woodstock. "Has anyone got any food we could give him?"

Jake and Nora shook their heads.

"I do," said Barnaby. He fished around in his pocket and brought out a cookie with cream inside.

"Is that all you ever eat?" Woodstock laughed.

Barnaby looked hurt. "I sometimes have shortbread cookies."

Jake took the cookie from Barnaby and waved it in the air.

"Here, Creature, have a nice cookie – OW!"

Creature had hurled a book down at him.

Nora took the cookie. "Creature, you really should eat something, you know," she called, holding the cookie up. She jumped back as another book was launched into the air.

"Silly thing! Can't you see we're trying to help you?" she cried.

"Let me try." Barnaby took the cookie back from Nora. He walked over to the bookcase. He didn't say anything, just held the cookie out on the palm of his hand.

Creature stopped twittering. He swung himself down until he was sitting on a shelf opposite Barnaby. Barnaby still didn't speak, just held the cookie out. Creature made a crooning noise, then reached out and took the cookie. He nibbled it happily. Barnaby withdrew his hand and looked smugly at the others, who were all staring at him.

"How come you're so good with him?" asked Nora.

Barnaby shrugged. "I've got five dogs at home. I'm good with animals."

"Five dogs?" Jake was doubtful.

"My mom loves dogs," said Barnaby. "She says they're nicer than people."

Creature finished the cookie and jumped on to Barnaby's shoulder.

"Can I take him home?" asked Barnaby, eagerly. "I promise I'll look after him."

Jake shook his head. "He's staying here tonight."

Barnaby looked disappointed. Nora looked at Jake.

"I don't think it's a good idea to leave him here," she said, slowly. "He'll cause chaos, and he might escape. I think you should take him home, Jake."

"Me?" Jake gulped. "Why not Barnaby? He wants to. And he's good with Creature."

"He's got five dogs. They might scare him."

"I'd take him, but my gran seriously would have a heart attack if she saw him," said Woodstock.

Jake sighed. *It was up to me, then.* He thought.

"Fine, I'll take him," he said. "Barnaby, you'd better show me what you did with that cookie."

RULE 9:
~~DO NOT~~ LEAVE YOUR
LITTLE SISTER IN CHARGE
OF A CREATURE

I'm late! The hallways were eerily empty as Jake hurtled towards the final corner before the classroom. *Where was everyone? And what was that clicking noise?*

He skidded around the corner.

CLICK! CLICK!

He screeched to a halt. A beetle as big as a rhino stood in front of the classroom door. It had dark hair and a painted-on, purple moustache.

Mrs. Blunt! She's turned into a giant beetle!

"JAKE JONES! Did you paint this moustache on me?" She lurched towards Jake, clicking her huge pincers threateningly. Jake tried to run but his legs turned to jelly . . .

He woke with a start.

Just a dream!

Maybe the whole thing with Creature was a dream, then? But — what's that on top of me?

Jake tried to sit up but couldn't. He peered over the covers.

"Jeeper-jeeper-jeeper!"

Groan. *Not a dream.* Creature was crouching on his chest, wearing Jake's Spiderman underwear on his head. When he saw Jake, he squeaked. Then he bounced off toward the door.

Somehow, Jake got there first.

"No you don't!" he exclaimed, slamming it shut. It burst open again.

"LOST MY TEDDY!"

Connie! His sister was only three but she was already nearly as big a pain as Amelia.

"Teddy. Not. Here," he grunted, trying to hold the door closed, but she bulldozed her way in, and spotted Creature.

"FUNNY DOGGY! CONNIE KISS DOGGY!" She waddled towards Creature with her chubby arms outstretched.

"Yik!" Creature made a face. Connie flung herself on him affectionately and yanked out a handful of fur. He squawked and ran into a corner. Connie shrieked in fury.

"DOGGY NO RUN 'WAY!"

She made a flying leap for Creature, grabbing his nose and nearly knocking his glasses off. That was the final straw. He hurled himself sideways, ran up the curtain, and perched on the curtain rail, trembling.

Jake had an idea.

"Connie — STAY HERE. I'll put *Best Dressed Pets* on, OK? Just don't leave the room . . ."

He grabbed some clothes from his wardrobe and managed to pull them on at the same time as sprinting to the TV and putting Connie's favorite show on. *She won't move now*, he thought, *and neither will Creature while she's in the room.* Then he ran to get breakfast. He sloshed milk over a bowl of cereal and was about to dash back upstairs but —

"Hello, Jake." Mom was blocking the doorway.

"Hi, Mom. I've just got to —"

"Why did you go straight up to your room yesterday?" His mom looked concerned. "Didn't you like your first day at school?"

"No, Mom, it's fine," Jake insisted. "I like it."

"Well, Granny was disappointed not to see you," his mother went on.

"Oh, sorry. I forgot Granny was staying over," Jake mumbled.

"Actually, she was supposed to be coming next week but she got her dates mixed up and —"

BRIIIIIIIIIIIIIING! The phone rang.

"For heaven's sake." Mom went to answer it.

Out of the corner of his eye, Jake spotted a small furry lightning bolt shoot past the kitchen door. Seconds later, Connie waddled past, crying.

“SILLY DOGGY! WON’T PUT DIAPER ON!”

Jake nearly dropped his cereal.

“Yes, Alan, the paperwork’s ready,” Mom was saying. Jake edged out of the kitchen unnoticed and ran down the hall. *Where’d Creature go?*

He heard a voice from the living room.

“Is that you, Jakey? Where’s my kiss?”

Granny!

He screeched to a halt outside the door.

“Have you grown a beard, dear? Goodness, children grow up fast these days!”

Puzzled, Jake pushed the door open.

Creature was squatting on Granny’s lap, puckering up his lips.

“NOOOOOOO!” yelled Jake. Creature shot straight upwards in fright and landed on the lampshade. Luckily Granny was quite deaf.

“What’s all this yelling?”

Jake whirled around. Dad walked in with a cup of tea. “It’s a madhouse here today. First Connie and now you. Here’s your tea, Mom —”

FAAARRRRRRTTTTTT!

An explosive fart noise erupted from the lampshade! Jake gulped. Dad would be sure to see Creature now! But he just put the tea down and frowned at Granny.

"Mom! Have you been eating baked beans? You know they don't agree with you."

Granny blinked. "Who doesn't agree with me?"

Dad shouted. "BAKED BEANS!"

"BAKE BEAN! BAKE BEAN!" Connie was in the doorway, laughing hysterically. Jake looked up for Creature. He'd vanished.

"David, did you open the front door?" he heard Mom call.

"No!" Dad shouted back. "More importantly, where are my car keys? They're not where I left them!"

Jake had a terrible thought. *Creature!* He shot to the window and pulled back the curtain.

Yup, there he was, trying to start the car! Jake pelted outside, past his startled dad, just in time to grab the keys. Creature chattered angrily and dove onto the back seat.

Dad appeared in the doorway. Jake held the keys out to him.

"Here are your keys, Dad. They were in the car."

"Were they, indeed?" Dad looked suspicious, but looked at his watch. "I've got to get going."

He got in the car and revved the engine.

Jake panicked: Creature was in the car. The car was rolling down the driveway!

"DAD!" Jake ran after it. Dad rolled the window down.

"Can you take me to school? I'm running late."

Dad rolled his eyes. "Be quick."

Phew. Jake ran indoors, grabbed Barnaby's bag, and ran out again. He jumped in the back. Creature was curled up asleep on the floor.

"Let's have the news," Dad said, switching the radio on. With some difficulty, Jake managed to stuff the sleeping Creature into the bag.

". . . on a lighter note, students at a local school are celebrating its fiftieth anniversary today with a special Founders' Celebration. The principal spoke to our reporter this morning."

"That's your school, Jake," said Dad. "Fame at last!"

Jake laughed weakly and did some quick counting. Six hours to go! And still no sign of Creature changing back . . .

Dad pulled up to the school gates just as the guard was closing them.

"Watch it!" the guard exclaimed as Jake swerved through, clutching the bag. He ran at breakneck speed across the empty playground, burst through the door . . .

SMACK!

. . . and crashed straight into Barnaby McCrumb.

RULE 10:
BOYS AND CREATURES
ARE ~~NOT~~ ALLOWED IN
THE GIRLS' BATHROOM

"Hi, Jake," said Barnaby, grinning. "I'll have my bag back now, thanks."

Jake gripped it. "No, Barnaby! Creature's asleep. You'll wake him up."

Barnaby grabbed the bag. "Come on, I want to see him!"

With a yank, Barnaby got the bag from Jake, but the weight took him by surprise and it fell to the floor with a thump.

"SQUAAAARK!"

The bag started lurching around violently.

"Now look what you've done," exclaimed Jake.

STOMP. STOMP. STOMP.

He froze. Footsteps were coming down the hallway. Jake and Barnaby looked at each other in panic. They had to hide Creature. But where?

"In here." Barnaby grabbed the bag and ran to the nearest door.

"That's the girls' bathroom!"

"We don't have a choice." Barnaby ran in. Jake followed him, heart hammering.

STOMP. STOMP.

Silence.

"Who's in there? You should be in class!" a familiar voice said loudly from right outside. "I'm the hall monitor, and I'm going to tell."

"It's Amelia," said Barnaby. "Get in a stall!"

They squeezed into the end stall and Barnaby put the bag on the toilet seat. Thankfully, Creature had gone quiet.

Creeeeeeeeeeeeeeeeaaak.

That was the door. Jake held his breath.

"You're in trouble now, whoever you are." Amelia's voice echoed around the bathroom.

Her footsteps came closer.

BANG!

Both boys jumped. They crouched down and peered under the door. Jake could see Amelia's feet walking along the row of stalls. She was banging each stall door open.

BANG! She was only two doors away.

There was a sudden noise above him. Jake glanced up, just in time to see Creature shoot out of the bag! He climbed gleefully over the stall wall, lost his grip, and tumbled into the next cubicle with a surprised squawk.

Jake froze. Within seconds, Amelia would open that door and see Creature!

"I know you're in there," Jake heard her hiss. He had to do something fast! He pushed Barnaby to one side and threw the cubicle door open. Too late.

BANG!

Creature shrieked.

“JEEPER-JEEPER-JEEPER-JEEPER-JEEPER!”

Jake saw Amelia’s face drain of color.

“BUUUUUUURRRRRRRRRRRRRRP!” Creature belched right in the trembling girl’s face.

Amelia screamed, “MOMMMMMMY!”

Then she collapsed in a heap on the floor.

“What’s happening?” asked Barnaby from inside the stall.

“Amelia saw Creature and fainted,” said Jake, running over to her. Barnaby came out.

"Great. She'll go straight to Mrs. Blunt," he said, looking down at her.

"We can't let her do that," said Jake. He thought frantically. "When she wakes up, we'll say it must have been a dream or something."

Amelia groaned. Creature was still bouncing around, squeaking.

"We have to get her out of here!" said Jake.

The two boys dragged Amelia out of the bathroom and into the hallway, propping her up against the wall.

"I'll stay with her. You go back in and get Creature in the bag again," said Jake.

Barnaby disappeared into the bathroom.

Amelia groaned again.

"Amelia!" Jake said in her ear. No response.

"WAKEY, WAKEY!" he said louder, shaking her shoulders. Her head shot up and her eyes popped open. She stared at Jake.

"The new boy!" she exclaimed. "What are you doing? Why am I here?"

"I heard a crash in the bathroom so I went to see what was happening," said Jake. "You must have fainted. You were dreaming, muttering something about a creature."

She stared at him. Then her face went pale.

"That wasn't a dream — there really was a monster! A nasty, smelly little monster . . .
it shouted 'jeeper-jeeper-jeeper' and burped at me . . . with horrid little eyes, and . . . and . . . it was wearing GLASSES!"

Jake put on a worried face.

"Monsters aren't real, Amelia," he said, patting her hand. "You've just had some sort of . . . of . . . dream or . . . or a hallucination or something."

Amelia pushed his hand away impatiently.

"Don't believe me? I'll show you!" she cried.

At that moment, Barnaby walked out of the bathroom with the bag over his shoulder. *Great timing, Barnaby*, Jake thought. *I should have warned him to stay put.*

Amelia's mouth dropped open.

"Barnaby McCrumb! What're you doing in the girls' bathroom?" she asked.

Barnaby shrugged. "I thought it was the boys'." He started to walk away.

"WAIT!" shouted Amelia. Barnaby stopped.

"There's . . . something . . . in the bathroom." Her voice faltered.

Barnaby grinned. "Sorry, it wouldn't flush."

Amelia stared at him in horror. "Ugh, I didn't mean that! I mean a monster!"

"Yes, it was, wasn't it," said Barnaby, grinning even more.

Amelia went bright red. She turned to Jake.

"New boy! Tell him what I saw."

"She saw a monster wearing glasses that said 'jeeper' and burped at her," said Jake.

Barnaby laughed. "Oh yeah, I saw it too." He deepened his voice. "Its Burp Power was strong, but mine was stronger, and I finally cast it down into the Bog of Beastliness for all Eternity."

Amelia glared at him. "You think you're so funny —"

Barnaby's bag suddenly squawked.

"JEEPER!"

Amelia's eyes nearly popped out.

"Did you hear that? That was it! *The monster!*" she cried.

The two boys looked at each other and shook their heads.

"I didn't hear anything," said Jake.

"Me neither," said Barnaby.

"You're still hallucinating," said Jake.

"Jeeper-jeeper-JEEPERRR!"

Amelia started shaking and pointed at the bag.

"It's in there — in your bag! It said 'jeeper-jeeper-jeeper'! You *must* have heard that!"

Barnaby looked at the bag. "Nah, it's just my gym clothes. They don't talk."

Jake had a sudden idea. He put on a concerned expression.

"Amelia, do you think you might need to go home, or see a doctor or something?"

Amelia went pale. "Why?"

"Well, you're clearly not very well, if you're imagining monsters. You probably shouldn't even do the Founders' Celebration tonight. It might just . . . tip you over the edge."

Amelia went paler. "I have to do it, I'm the Star of the Show!"

Barnaby got the hint. He shook his head sadly.

"Mrs. Blunt would definitely say not to —"

"*What* would I definitely say not to do?"

Mrs. Blunt was standing not three yards away, with a face like thunder.

Jake and Barnaby shuffled awkwardly. Amelia staggered to her feet.

"Mrs. B-B-Blunt," she stammered.

"Amelia? Are you all right?"

"I'm fine, ma'am!" squeaked Amelia. "I'm really . . . excited about to the Founders' Celebration tonight!"

Mrs. Blunt looked closely at Amelia. Then at Barnaby. Then at Jake.

"If you don't tell me what's happening," she said coldly, "you boys will both be working on the Rockery all day."

Jake felt his heart thumping painfully. One false move, and he could give the whole game away. He had to say something, though.

"Well, ma'am . . . Amelia says she saw something . . ."

Amelia yelped. "I didn't see anything, ma'am, I'm really fine!"

She's desperate to perform at the Founders' Celebration, thought Jake.

Mrs. Blunt fixed Jake with a stare. "What did Amelia see?"

Out of the corner of his eye, Jake saw Barnaby suddenly shift nervously and shove the bag behind him with his foot. Mrs. Blunt saw.

"What's in that bag?"

Barnaby gulped and shook his head wildly.

"It's just my gym clothes, ma'am!"

"It just moved! Let me see."

She darted around Barnaby and grabbed one of the handles. Barnaby yelped.

"Mrs. Blunt, I really wouldn't! It's a bit stinky! It hasn't been washed for a year!"

Jake chimed in. "It's disgusting. It's actually growing things."

Barnaby nodded. "I'm giving it to Nora to do some experiments on. She thinks there are life forms in there that exist nowhere else on the planet."

Mrs. Blunt dropped the bag handle as if it had burned her. Then she looked at the white-faced Amelia, and shook her head.

"Poor child," she said. "Come with me."

She started walking Amelia down the hallway.

"No one should have to witness Barnaby McCrumb's dirty gym clothes."

As Jake and Barnaby walked into the classroom, the buzz of voices died away. Karl was strumming a guitar, but he stopped when he saw them. All eyes turned to Barnaby and the bag.

Nora's face fell. "Is he still Creature?"

Jake nodded glumly. A disappointed murmur ran around the room.

"Better let him out, Barnaby," Jake said. Barnaby unzipped the bag.

For a moment nothing happened, then Creature's dishevelled head appeared. He squawked, shot out of the bag, and headed straight for the fish tank, where he stuck his head under the water and started blowing raspberries at the fish.

"Oh, leave them alone, Creature," Nora said. But she didn't move.

Creature pulled his head out and shook it, spraying water everywhere. Then he bounded

across desks and jumped on to Mr. Hyde's chair. He grabbed a pen, cackled, and started scrawling "CREATURE WOZ ERE" all over the whiteboard.

The class sat in gloomy silence. No one had the heart to try and stop him.

Nora sighed. “And don’t forget — we’ve got to rehearse ‘The Joy of School Rules’ for tonight.”

Woodstock groaned. “‘The Joy of School Rules?’ That’s a joke! More like ‘The School Rules Blues.’”

Karl strummed a chord.

“I got the School Rules Blues,” he sang, softly. “I’m in trouble again . . .”

As Karl started playing, Jake happened to glance at Creature. Something very strange happened.

Creature stopped scrawling on the board and began swaying to the music, a dreamy look on his face. As soon as the music stopped, the dreamy look vanished and he started cackling again.

That's it!

"Karl!" shouted Jake. "Play that again!"

Karl looked questioningly at Jake.

"It did something to Creature!"

Karl started strumming again.

"I got the School Rules Blues, I'm in trouble again . . ."

Creature stopped scrawling and looked at Karl. Then he looked at Jake and squeaked.

He wants me to join in! Jake thought.

Jake snapped his fingers. Creature made a soft clicking sound and looked at the rest of the class. It dawned on Jake. *Not just me — everyone!*

"Everyone. Join in!" he called.

The class looked hesitantly at each other. Jake felt desperate. He knew this was going to work. It *had* to work! But how to get everyone working together?

"Wa-ah-wa-ah-womp-womp!
Chuppa-chuppa-chomp-chomp!
Doo-wup doo-wup a diddy-dum-
diddy-doo!"

Was that drums? Jake spun around.

The drum noises were coming from Barnaby's mouth! Jake watched, amazed. It sounded just like real drums and cymbals!

Barnaby's a human beatbox!

Karl played faster, in time with Barnaby's beatboxing. It was impossible not to tap your feet, and before Jake knew it, everyone was clapping in time!

"I got the School Rules Bluuuues, I'm in trouble agaaaain . . ." sang Karl.

Alexis ran to join him.

"I got a Creature for a teacher . . ." she sang.

Woodstock looked up. "And it's driving me insane . . ."

"I'm just trying to do my lessons . . ." sang Nora, adjusting her glasses.

"He's trying to climb up the drain!" Jake finished the verse, grinning.

Karl and Barnaby carried on playing, and one by one, everyone joined in, singing a line each, and grabbing things to beat out the rhythm — pens, pencils, rulers — whatever was on hand.

Jake got so into it that he almost forgot Creature — but not quite.

He looked back to the front of the class.

Creature had hopped onto the teacher's desk and was crooning softly, completely wrapped up in the music. His eyes glowed behind his glasses, getting brighter and brighter. His whole body started to light up with a trembling orange glow and every hair on his body stood on end. The music faltered as the class gawked in astonishment.

"Keep going!" Jake shouted.

Everyone sang together. "We got the School Rules Blues . . ."

Creature was now a blazing ball of brightness so intense it was painful to look at him. A pile of papers where he was resting smoldered and burst into flames.

"I'm in trouble again . . ."

"JEEPERRRR-RRR-RR!"

The glowing ball of Creature let out a deafening war cry and swung himself under the teacher's desk.

The room went dark.

". . . Creature . . . for a . . . teacher . . ." the voices wavered. The music died away. A loud, steady noise was coming from under the desk.

Nora covered her ears. Jake covered his eyes. Barnaby covered his lunch box.

FAAAAAAAAAAARRRRT!

Wheeeeeeee . . . .

POP! POP! POP!

BANG!

RULE 12:
DON'T YOU REMEMBER
RULE 11? I SAID ~~NO PLAYING~~
PLAY THAT FUNKY MUSIC
~~OF POPULAR MUSIC!~~

Twenty-six pairs of eyes were focused on the teacher's desk.

For a moment, nothing happened. Then the desk shuddered. Then there was a groan.

"MR. HYDE!" cried Nora, jumping to her feet.

It worked! Jake breathed a sigh of relief and beat out the flames that had ignited the papers.

It was, indeed, Mr. Hyde. He stood up. His hair was wild and his glasses were crooked, but apart from that he looked exactly as he had looked before he changed into Creature.

There was a cheer.

"Are you all right, sir?" cried Nora, running up to him.

Mr. Hyde gazed around as if unsure of where he was. He straightened his glasses and focused on Nora.

"Oh dear," he said. "Please tell me that what I *think* just happened *didn't* happen?"

Nora looked uncertain. "I think it did happen, sir. Sorry to have to say it."

Mr. Hyde sat down heavily on his chair.

"What did I do?" he asked in a dismal voice.

There was a pause.

"Um . . . you ate paint," said Woodstock.

"You gave Mrs. Blunt a purple moustache," called Karl.

"You tried to kiss my granny," added Jake.

Mr. Hyde winced.

"OK — I've heard enough," he said sadly. "I owe you an explanation."

The students leaned forward expectantly.

"A few years ago, I started having strange dreams," Mr. Hyde began. "At first I didn't take any notice — they were just dreams, right? In these dreams, I would turn into a creature. Sometimes large, sometimes small. Always badly-behaved."

"You were some sort of monkey," said Alexis.

"Crossed with a Tasmanian Devil," added Nora.

He nodded. "That's what it usually is. After a while I noticed that when I woke up my back door was open and the neighbors' gardens had been turned upside down. Then I realized the dreams I'd been having *weren't* dreams. They were actually happening!"

"Weren't you scared?" whispered Nora, eyes wide.

Mr. Hyde nodded. "Of course. I locked all my doors and windows at night to stop myself getting out. But it got worse. I started changing in the middle of the day."

"What makes you change?" asked Jake. "Is it when you get angry?"

"Angry, sad, happy — any strong emotion can set it off. I never know how long it'll last, or what I'm going to do." He looked at the class, suddenly anxious. "You won't say anything to anyone, will you? They'd send in scientists, hook me up to things . . ."

"NO!" everyone exclaimed.

"We won't, sir. We already agreed to that," said Jake. Mr. Hyde looked relieved.

"Well, I'm glad I changed back before I did anything really awful," he said. "Jake, I wish I could apologize to your granny."

Karl had been bursting to speak.

"Sir . . . music changed you back. We wrote an awesome song for you."

Mr. Hyde looked at him. "Really?" he said. "I'd love to hear it —" He stopped and smiled sadly. "But I don't think you'll be wanting a creature for a teacher. I'm sorry, 5B, but I'm going to hand in my resignation."

He stood up and walked toward the door.

Every student in the class jumped up.

"NO!"

Jake shot to the door and blocked his way.

"You can't leave," Jake said firmly. "You're a great teacher!"

"The best," added Woodstock.

"Your dancing was . . . inspiring," said Karl.

"Your solar system was amazing!" said Nora.

"Your moon rock cakes were delicious," said Barnaby, grinning.

Mr. Hyde blinked. "Do you . . . do you really mean that?"

"YES!" everyone shouted.

Mr. Hyde scratched his head. "I suppose I could give it another try."

"HURRAY!" Everyone cheered. Mr. Hyde's face went red and he grinned happily.

"You really are the best class in the world! I better do some teaching then, huh? What's on the menu for today's learning extravaganza?"

Nora and Jake exchanged looks.

"We have to practice for the Founders' Celebration tonight," said Jake, grimacing.

Mr. Hyde clapped his hands. "Of course! 'The Joy of School Rules.' OK, everyone in position! Hop to it, folks!" Mr. Hyde bounded around, moving tables. He stopped, and looked around. "What's the problem?"

There was silence.

Woodstock plucked up courage. "Sir, no one wants to do the poem."

Karl nodded. "It's s-o-o-ooo boring."

"No one can remember the words," said Alexis.

"Plus it's factually inaccurate," added Nora.

Mr. Hyde scratched his head. "I see your point. But we have to do something."

Karl put his hand up. "We could do our song!"

Mr. Hyde's eyes twinkled. "The song that made me change back? Excellent idea! Let's hear it then."

"Yessss!" Karl grabbed his guitar and marched to the front. "Ready, Barnaby? Everyone? 'THE SCHOOL RULES BLUES!'"

Jake and his friends began to sing just like they did before. Then the whole class joined in the chorus:

"We got the School Rules Blues,
But that's not going to bring us down!
We've got a Creature for a teacher,
He's small and furry and brown . . .
There ain't no teacher like him —
He's the best teacher in town!"

The last chord rang out. Mr. Hyde sat stock still. Everyone shuffled nervously.

Then he leapt up, clapping furiously.

"JEEPERS! That was amazing! Karl, hats off to you — and Barnaby, extraordinary! All of you — you rock!"

"Can we do it at the Founders' Celebration, then, sir?" asked Nora.

Mr. Hyde laughed. "Of course! People are going to love it! We'll have to change some of the words, of course."

All excited, everyone started talking. But something was bothering Jake. He beckoned to Barnaby.

"What about Amelia?" he whispered. "What if she changes her mind and says something about Creature in the girls' bathroom?"

Barnaby winked. "Leave Amelia to me."

RULE 13:
ALWAYS
~~DO NOT~~ SNORE
DURING SCHOOL
PERFORMANCES

"Drive faster, Dad!" urged Jake. They were horribly late because Connie had hidden the car keys in the toilet.

"We're stuck in a traffic jam, Jake," said Dad.

Jake's mom pointed. "The sidewalks are jammed too. They must all be going to the Founders' Celebration!"

Jake looked out. It was true — everyone was heading for the school. His stomach lurched at the thought of being on stage in front of all those people. As the car inched closer to the gates, he spotted Nora just outside them.

"Stop the car, Dad. I'll get out here." Jake jumped out.

"Break a leg!" his dad called, as he drove off.

Nora rolled her eyes as he ran over to her. "Where've you been? Mr. Hyde told me to come and find you!"

"When are we on?" asked Jake as they headed through the gates.

"Second – after 5A. We've got about twenty minutes."

Diving between swarms of twitchy parents, they raced through the gates and down the hallway to the changing room. As they burst through the changing room doors, a deafening wall of noise hit Jake's ears.

"Who's on first?"

"I've lost my wings!"

"Where are those pesky ants?"

Nora beckoned to Jake. "This way."

Mr. Hyde was giving Class 5B a pep talk as they approached.

"Remember, you are winners! Repeat after me: WE ARE WINNERS!"

Class 5B mumbled: "We are winners . . ."

"Again! WE – Ah, Jake and Nora," said Mr. Hyde. "Are we all here now? Where's Barnaby?"

Jake looked around. Barnaby was nowhere to be seen.

Nora frowned. "He was here earlier."

"We can't do it without him!" exclaimed Karl.

The loudspeaker in the corner crackled.

"FIVE MINUTE CALL FOR CLASS 5A. 5A, TAKE YOUR POSITIONS BACKSTAGE!"

Mr. Hyde stood up. "We'd better go too. We're on after 5A. Don't worry, Barnaby will show up."

They trooped out of the changing room to the backstage area. It was jam-packed with fidgeting, whispering students. Jake looked around for Barnaby, with no luck. He bit his lip. Karl was right — the song wouldn't work without Barnaby and his beatboxing. *Where could he be?*

Suddenly, he heard a sharp, bossy voice over the hushed whispers.

"Not like that, Kaylee! Pin it *higher*. No, higher, I said! And Sonia, you didn't fix my antenna on properly, they keep slipping off!"

Amelia, thought Jake, wincing. He looked around. Yup, there she was, flouncing about in her humongous, horrid pink and yellow butterfly costume. Her two friends, in bee costumes, were fussing around her while she yelled orders at them.

"Where's my water?" she screeched. "Someone bring me water!" A ladybug scuttled off for water.

"I know what I'd do with that water," he heard a whisper in his ear. "Pour it over her head." It was Woodstock.

Jake grinned at him."Yeah, me too."

They both chuckled.

"Let's go and wait in the wings," said Woodstock. "You can see the audience from there."

They wormed through the mass of students to the side of the stage, pulled the curtain back a tiny bit, and peered out. Jake scanned the crowd for his parents and spotted them near the back. *Mom looks nervous*. He gulped. *We have to get this right!*

The buzz of voices died away as Mrs. Blunt climbed the steps and clicked across the front of the stage in the highest heels Jake had ever seen.

There was a soft "pop" as she turned the microphone on.

"Welcome, everyone. This evening, we are delighted to welcome our esteemed Founders —"

ZZZZZ- Z- Z- Z- Z- Z- Z . . .

A loud snore interrupted Mrs. Blunt's speech. She stopped, flustered.

Jake peered around the curtain and saw four incredibly old people sitting in the front row. Two men and two women, silver-haired and as wrinkled and grumpy as rhinoceroses.

"The esteemed Founders," whispered Woodstock. Jake tried not to giggle.

One of the Founders was fast asleep, with his mouth wide open. It was from here that the snore had erupted.

"Wake up, Harold!" said the woman next to him, whacking him over the head with her handbag. He woke up and looked around.

"What's that, dear?" he asked. "Supper's ready, you say?" and then went straight back to sleep.

Mrs. Blunt continued between gritted teeth.

"*. . . to welcome our esteemed Founders, who established this school fifty years ago on such excellent rules . . .*"

ZZZZ-Z-Z-Z-Z-Z-Z . . .

Jake thought, by the look on Mrs. Blunt's face, she was probably at this very moment devising Rule 143: "No Snoring During School Performances." Grinning, he turned to share this thought with Woodstock, but Woodstock suddenly clutched Jake's shoulder and gasped.

"What —?" Jake began, but then he stopped and stared across the stage.

Barnaby was loitering in the wings on the other side of the stage. He was talking to Amelia, who was smirking and handing a bag to Barnaby.

Jake gasped too. "She's giving him candy!"

"Quick, we've got to stop her!" said Woodstock.

Jake and Woodstock started fighting their way across the sea of Class 5A insects, who were all pushing and shoving to get ready to go on.

"Barnaby!" called Jake across the sea of heads, but Barnaby didn't hear. Amelia held the bag out . . . Barnaby reached out his hand . . .

"We're too late," panted Woodstock. They finally reached Barnaby. He saw them, and winked. Then he pushed the bag of candy away.

Puzzled, Amelia stared at the bag, then at Barnaby.

"Go on — they're your faves." She held the bag out again.

Barnaby shook his head and grinned at her.

"Seen any monsters recently, Amelia?"

"Wha-what?"

"JEEPER-JEEPER-JEEPER!" Barnaby hissed.

Amelia froze. The color drained from her face, and the bag dropped from her hand. It landed on the floor with a thud and burst, sending hundreds of little round candies rolling everywhere.

Barnaby grinned. Then he opened his mouth.

"BUUUUUURRRRRPPPP!"

"YOU? *You're* the m-m-monster?" stammered Amelia.

RULE 14:
WHEN THINGS GO
PANIC!
WRONG, ~~REMAIN CALM~~

Amelia backed away from Barnaby toward the stage, a look of terror on her face.

"*. . . to start us off, Class 5A, performing The Butterfly Ball . . .*" Mrs. Blunt was saying.

Barnaby took a step toward Amelia.

He burped again.

"*. . . starring the exceptionally talented Amelia Trotter-Hogg!*" declared Mrs. Blunt.

With a shriek, Amelia backed right onto the stage, in full view of the audience. As she did so, her feet hit some of the rolling candies and shot out from under her. Jake watched, open-mouthed, as the exceptionally talented Amelia Trotter-Hogg flew across the stage in

a not-very-butterfly-like way and skidded smack into Mrs. Blunt!

Mrs. Blunt tottered, swayed, then fell off the stage . . .

WHUMP!

. . . landing on top of the snoring Harold, whose mouth was still wide open. As she did so, his false teeth shot out and attached themselves to Mrs. Blunt's nose. Jake, Barnaby, and Woodstock, peering around the curtain, nearly died laughing.

"HELP! I'm being attacked!" squawked Harold. Harold's wife, who had also fallen asleep during Mrs. Blunt's speech, woke up.

"Get off my husband!" she shrieked. She began bashing the red-faced Mrs. Blunt over the head with her handbag.

"Ow! Sorry! Ow!" squeaked Mrs. Blunt, fending off blows. She managed to disentangle herself from Harold and crawl away from the frenzied handbag attack, Harold's false teeth still firmly attached to her nose. She ripped them off, looked around wildly, and then shouted at the pianist.

"Music, Mavis!"

The startled pianist launched into a song. Amelia staggered to her feet, flapping her wings weakly. As the two bees buzzed onstage, the pianist realized she was playing the wrong music and stopped. The confused bees tried to retreat, but got caught in a spider-web prop, where they hung, thrashing and squealing.

Finally, the pianist found the right music but started playing at double speed. Amelia tried to keep up, but she flapped so fast one of her wings fell off. The front end of the caterpillar had an argument with the back end, and broke in half. Meanwhile, the ants milled around getting in everyone's way.

Jake could not believe his eyes. It was chaos. And out of all the students on stage, Amelia was the worst. *Even Connie could do better*, he thought. The Founders clearly weren't impressed either.

"What *is* this?" asked one.

"Some modern silliness," said another.

"It wouldn't have happened in *my* day," snapped Harold's wife, waving her handbag menacingly in Mrs. Blunt's direction.

Finally, The Butterfly Ball fizzled out. There were a few nervous claps as Class 5A shuffled off stage. Jake, Woodstock, and Barnaby looked at each other.

"We're on now," whispered Woodstock, looking pale.

"Remember, folks — WE ARE WINNERS!"

Jake turned around. Mr. Hyde and the rest of Class 5B were right behind him.

On stage, a flustered Mrs. Blunt took the microphone.

"*Thank you, 5A. A very, errm . . . interesting performance . . . anyway, who's next? Oh yes, Class 5B, reciting a poem written by me.*" She beckoned frantically to Mr. Hyde. ". . . afraid they've not had much time to practice . . ." she was saying as Mr. Hyde led the class onstage. Jake looked out into a sea of expectant faces. He swallowed, his mouth suddenly dry. *This is it.*

Mr. Hyde took the microphone.

"You're right, Mrs. Blunt, they haven't had much time," he said, "but they're a very talented bunch of kids, and I know they'll give a performance to remember. Ready, everyone?"

Karl stood up, guitar in hand."One, two, *one-two-three-four!*"

He launched into the song. Jake felt his foot start tapping.

"We got the School Rules Blues . . .
Every boy and every girl . . ."

There were hoots and whistles from the audience as Barnaby started to beatbox. A few people started clapping to the rhythm.

"We got a brand new teacher . . .
He's really out of this world . . ."

As Jake sang his line he caught a glimpse of his mom and dad grinning and waving enthusiastically at the back. A stream of crazy

rhythms flew out of Barnaby's mouth, Nora and Alexis danced wildly, and Karl played a fantastic guitar break. By the last verse, the whole audience was clapping, whistling, and dancing. Even the Founders were tapping their feet!

Mrs. Blunt wasn't clapping, whistling, or dancing. She had her arms crossed, a look of fury on her face. As the last chord rang out, she stalked onstage.

"I'm sorry . . . this was not my poem —"

"BRAVO!"

Jake blinked. *Who was that?*

Harold! The elderly Founder was on his feet, clapping excitedly. Mrs. Blunt paused, confused.

"There's been a mistake —" she began.

"ENCORE!" Harold's wife was standing too, waving her handbag.

Mrs. Blunt's mouth opened and closed like a fish out of water.

"BRAVO! ENCORE!"

Everyone was on their feet, shouting for more! Jake and his classmates looked at each other, excited and full of energy.

We did it, Jake thought proudly.

"ENCORE!" the crowd roared.

Mrs. Blunt looked as if she might collapse.

"Well . . . maybe . . . just this once . . ." she said faintly.

Mr. Hyde smiled and turned to the audience.

"Ladies and gentlemen, let's hear it again for the Fabulous 5B Band!" He strode to the piano. "I'll join you on piano. Take it away, Karl!"

In a daze, they started to play, with the audience singing along. Mr. Hyde was an incredible pianist, and captivated the crowd instantly. The spotlight swivelled to focus on him. He played faster and faster, till his hands were a blur.

Jake stared. Something wasn't quite right.

Was smoke coming off the keys? It smelled funny, almost like . . . burning rubber! That spotlight was way too bright! Jake shielded his eyes . . . *Oh no!*

It wasn't the spotlight. Mr. Hyde was glowing! He glowed brighter and brighter, till even the tips of his hair crackled.

Beside Jake, Nora gasped. Jake jumped up.

"Quick!" he shouted. "The curtains!"

Jake and Nora sprinted to the curtains and pulled them across, just as Mr. Hyde disappeared in an explosion of white light!

Jake took the microphone.

He bowed. "That's all folks! Thank you, and good —"

"BUUUUURRRRRPPP!"

ABOUT THE AUTHOR

Sam Watkins voraciously consumed books from a young age, due to a food shortage in the village where she grew up. This diet, although not recommended by doctors, has given her a lifelong passion for books. She has been a bookseller, editor, and publisher, and writes and illustrates her own children's books. At one point, things all got a bit too bookish so she decided to be an art teacher for a while, but books won the day in the end.

ABOUT THE ILLUSTRATOR

David O'Connell is an illustrator who lives in London, England. His favorite things to draw are monsters, naughty children (another type of monster), batty old ladies, and evil cats . . . Oh, and teachers that transform into naughty little creatures!

GLOSSARY

bicker (BIK-ur) — to argue about small things

croon (kroon) — to hum or sing in a low, soft voice

doubtful (DOUT-ful) — full of doubts; uncertain

focus (FOH-kuhs) — to give attention to something or somebody

gaggle (GA-guhl) — an unorganized group

laboratory (LAB-ruh-tor-ee) — a place that has special equipment for doing scientific experiments and tests

petrified (PET-ruh-fide) — so scared that you are unable to move; stunned

snicker (SNIK-ur) — a mean or disrespectful laugh

TALK ABOUT IT!

1. At the end of the story, the kids made sure nobody saw Mr. Hyde turn into Creature on stage. Phew! That was a close one! Tell someone what you think happened to Creature and class 5B after the curtains closed.
2. Mrs. Blunt and Mr. Hyde have very different personalities. Can you think of all their differences? Talk with someone about these two characters.
3. Music makes Mr. Hyde very happy. It always seems to put him in a great mood! What puts you in a good mood? Talk about it with a friend and see if you have anything in common.
4. Class 5B sings a blues song about Mr. Hyde. There are all kinds of musical styles. Talk with your friends about their favorite songs and music. If you want to learn about a new musical style, go to the library and ask for help from the librarian.

WRITE ABOUT IT!

1. Nora's treehouse is her Top Secret hideout. If you could make your very own hideout, where would it be? How would it look? What would you do inside? Write down all the details, make some sketches, and keep your report in a Top Secret folder!

2. In the story, different characters act as leaders. Which characters are good leaders, and why do you think so? Which characters are not good leaders, and why?

3. Nora is great at science, Woodstock is skilled at drawing, and Barnaby is good at beatboxing. Write about your friends, and list all their skills and talents!

4. Class 5B really likes Mr. Hyde. Do you have a favorite teacher? Think about all the reasons you like your teacher. Then, write him or her a thank you letter and deliver it.